DISNEY DESCENDANTS 2

EVIE'S FASHION BOOK

Based on the film by Josann McGibbon and Sara Parriott

Adapted by Tina McLeef

Printed in the United States of America

First Hardcover Edition, July 2017

1 3 5 7 9 10 8 6 4 2

FAC-038091-17153

Library of Congress Control Number: 2017934289

ISBN 978-1-368-00251-6

For more Disney Press fun, visit www.disneybooks.com

Visit DisneyChannel.com

EVIE'S FASHION BOOK

DISNEY PRESS

LOS ANGELES • NEW YORK

I've been thinking of everything that happened the night of Cotillion, and all the magic (and mayhem) surrounding it. My friends and I have only been in Auradon a little while, but so much has changed for all of us. Mal is officially lady of the court; Carlos truly learned how to speak up for himself, and is also dating Jane; and Jay is learning how to bend the rules, not break them.

And me? The biggest thing for me is that I started my Evie's 4 Hearts business, designing couture gowns and ready-to-wear school outfits for Auradon Prep students. What started small is now a huge operation—Doug helps me, and I may need to hire real employees soon. There are just too many orders to keep up with. And I have a real boyfriend (no more crushing on that goofball Chad). Doug's a true prince charming and one of the best people I've ever met.

AND I have this sketchbook back! My old sketchbook from the Isle! I made this "fairest" outfit sketch when I was living there, using old materials to create my looks. My friend Dizzy who lives there saved it for me. More on her later. . . .

Red leather piping on edges of
sleeves, to offset the blue

Ruffled edge on neckline

short skirt—tulle??

Gold crown-shaped pockets

Jewels, jewels, and more jewels

Fashion Rules for the Isle of the Lost

Do:

Look intimidating

Have your own unique style

Remember "bad" is good

Wear something you can run, duck, and cover in

Make sure your clothes are durable and tough

Don't:

Ask anyone where they got their clothes (people hate that)

Loan anyone anything you like (you probably won't get it back)

Plan on keeping your outfit too clean

Expect any compliments

Use the coat check—it's a scam

This is another design I came up with back on the Isle. It obviously inspired the outfit I created for Mal's meeting with Aladdin and Jasmine. It was fun to make this dress in Auradon, where I have access to so many unique materials and fabrics.

Gold ribbon detail throughout

Sheer fabric with pattern

Hand-stamped?

Handkerchief-type hem

Uneven neckline, or single sleeve, with drape

Sheer fabric with shine

Even though there would never be a royal ball on the Isle, a girl can dream. If I ever get to go to one, I'm going to wear the biggest, poufiest dress I can make. The skirt will have a long train on the back, and I'll reinforce the underside so it comes out in all directions.

DREAM BALLGOWN

One-shoulder neckline

Red velvet bow
at waist

Floor-length,
many-tiered
skirt made of
various fabrics
for lots of
volume

♡ one day...

Finding Fabulous Materials

My mom was in a major eyebrow-tweezing mood, so I decided to go scavenging for new materials. I found so many interesting and unique things in alleyways and even in the trash (gross, but worth it!). Some of them I might use for jewelry, but others I can incorporate into my clothing designs.

Old ribbons and strips of fabric: I can decorate blouses with these or use them as laces in my boots. (Combat boots look awesome with a bright velvet or frilly white lace!)

Nuts and bolts: these might look cool on a pair of boots

Sea glass: great for pendants and earrings

Peacock feathers: for the back of a coat?

Old keys and locks: I love these for necklaces and bracelets

A mouse skull: I want to paint this gold and glue it on a ring

STYLE TIP

"Found items" can totally personalize your clothes.

— Collect different types of buttons and then swap out the plain ones that come on your clothes with more interesting options.

— A lone dangly earring can be transformed into a great necklace pendant if you take off the earring part and run a ribbon or leather strip through the leftover loop.

— Broken chains, strips of fabric, denim or lace, and even old pieces of wire can be braided together to make a cool bracelet— try a combination of elements.

Scavenging for materials back on the Isle was fun, and I still love to hunt for unique trimmings and notions in little shops outside of town.

But I have to say, the materials I get to use here in Auradon are BEYOND. Today I got another shipment in—boxes and boxes of every color fabric, all just waiting for me to cut them up and turn them into something beautiful. Silks and lace, satins and tweeds. The supplies come from all over, sent from craftsmen deep in the heart of Sherwood Forest or quaint little shops in Camelot Heights.

Life in Auradon is good—no, it's better than good. I could never have imagined how many opportunities I'd have here. I'm so happy Dizzy saved this old sketchbook from the Isle. It's a piece of my former life there and it reminds me of who I am and where I came from.

. . . But I'm also really proud of how far I've come. And I'm going to fill the rest of this book with everything I've done since getting to Auradon—my latest design sketches, photos, ideas, and inspiration. I'm even going to add some fashion tips!

Get ready for

FIERCE FASHION
BY EVIE

a.k.a.

EVIE'S 4 HEARTS

Turn for more →

I design everything from ready-to-wear school outfits to Cotillion couture gowns. This is one of my school looks, and by far my most versatile design. I wear it for fittings, to class, or to dinner with Doug. The royal blue cotton has a little stretch to it, which makes it incredibly comfortable.

My Blue Sheath Dress

Silver and blue beading at collar

Paired with red fingerless gloves

FLARED SKIRT

Fitted to hips

Royal blue cotton has a subtle pattern to it

STYLE TIP ♡ ♡ ♡

Statement belts really bring an outfit together and create a nice waistline. Wear one to cinch a voluminous shirt, or even over a long cardigan!

Belts with a lot of embellishments go best with solid-colored clothing.

Patent Leather Boots

I bought these at a boutique in Auradon, but they were so plain. I ordered different charms and jewels from a vendor in Seaside to decorate them with.

How to:

Buy some super inexpensive boots and hit up a sewing store for charms to add on. Try a pattern or add them randomly—both ways look cool! (Just make sure to use a strong glue!)

Gold heart pendants

Gold and diamond crowns

GOLD HEEL

Red and gold jeweled hearts

TIARA

Red jeweled hearts

GOLD CROWN

What can I say? Nothing screams EVIE like a tiara. I hand-glued every jewel onto this myself.

YEAR-TO-DATE EARNINGS:

22 SILVER COINS
2 RUBIES
5 SAPPHIRES
13 GOLD COINS
46 BRONZE COINS

THE BUSINESS IS PROJECTED TO GROW
BY 160 PERCENT IN THE NEXT YEAR
AND 450 PERCENT IN THE FOLLOWING
TWO YEARS.

Evie, this is incredible!
Let's discuss investing
your profit.

—Doug

The Story Behind Evie's 4 Hearts

I've been designing clothes forever. I remember when I was little, using my mom's old cloak and wrapping it around my body three times, making this really cool off-the-shoulder black dress.

It wasn't until I came to Auradon, though, that I finally realized my talent could be a business. My friends and I had chosen good over evil, and that day at the coronation ceremony changed everything. We stood there and recited the words: "The strength of evil is as good as none, when stands before four hearts as one." It's funny . . . even weeks after the ceremony, I couldn't help thinking about those words, and my friends, and all we'd accomplished together. I'd stay up late, sewing a jacket for Carlos or making a one-of-a-kind purse for Mal, and I'd think: "Four hearts. Wouldn't that be a great name for a fashion label?"

At first I just made things for me and my friends. I made Carlos this cool fake fur accent to hang off his pants. I made Mal a dress for her dinner with Aladdin and Jasmine. I made Jay a jacket for school. And, as always, I was dressed head to toe in my designs. Every earring, every scarf—even my shoes were Evie's 4 Hearts original items. It wasn't long before people started to notice.

I'd get compliments on my jacket, and a girl would ask me where I'd gotten it. Everyone seemed shocked when I said I had made it. It wasn't long before girls (and even some guys) were stopping by my room, wondering if they could buy some of my Evie's 4 Hearts clothing. I started working a few hours every day after school and then, when I got more orders, I asked Doug to help me keep track of everything—the shipments, payments, production fees, everything. Now I work before school, after school, and on weekends. Cotillion more than doubled my orders. Doug just ran the numbers the other day, and he said the way business is going, I'll have enough money to buy a castle one day. My very own castle. Can you believe that?!

My Favorite Skirt

Sure, this took me a full week to make, but it turned out to be beautiful. I hand-painted royal blue tulle with different designs, then layered the tulle to create fullness.

Striped fitted bodice

Glitter paint adds sparkle

FIFTEEN LAYERS OF TULLE!

EDGY PREP

Easy Ways to Mix Auradon and Isle Style:

Sweet fabrics like tulle + fierce boots

Girly skirts paired with edgy accessories

Tiaras and leather

A mid-length skirt is an essential! Pair it with flat boots and a T-shirt for a casual look, or with heels and a blouse for a dressier event or evening out.

I throw this jacket over everything—dresses, T-shirts, silk blouses, or jumpsuits. Because most of my wardrobe has blue in it, the cherry red goes with almost everything. Bonus: it's super warm on cold nights.

RED CROPPED JACKET

I added this at the last minute. Hearts and crowns are part of my signature style, so I made this design on the back.

These charms came from a bracelet I found at an Auradon boutique. I took it apart and sewed the pieces onto the back.

Leather details at the shoulders?

FRONT OF JACKET: Asymmetrical zippers Studded collar

I call this deconstruct + reconstruct!

STYLE TIP ♡ ♡ ♡

If you're going to spend extra money on a special item, a jacket is a great investment. Save up for a versatile jacket that goes with everything. It doesn't have to be leather—satin, denim, and pleather are all great options.

Royal Blue Silk Dress

Wear with heart choker necklace

ASYMMETRICAL SEAMS

Royal blue raw silk

High-low skirt (shorter in front and longer in back)

Gold chain strap

Red Patent Leather Boots:

Chunky heels

Subtle silver detail at zipper

Rounded toe

Red satin fabric for the heart

Clasp Purse

The rhinestones were imported from South Riding

These boots are sleek and simple, so I can pair them with anything.

My Isle Look

Red leather piping on collar

Gold studs on the shoulders

ASYMMETRICAL ZIPPERS ON FRONT OF JACKET

Removable studded sleeves

Red leather heart detail at the waist, to offset the blue

GOLD ACCENTS HAND-PAINTED ONTO LEGGINGS

Jewels, studs, embellishments!

This took me a while to create. I hand-sewed every piece, right down to the gloves. I couldn't decide if I wanted a skirt or leggings, so I did both. It's the ultimate layered look.

This jacket can transition through the seasons.

Long sleeves attach with hidden zippers underneath cap sleeves

Don't Throw Shade

It's all good if a lot of your clothes are the same color—you probably feel comfortable and happy wearing it. I love blue and wear it all the time! As they say, you do you.

ISLE LOOK —NO JACKET

Hand-painted heart and crown

Rips at hem and neckline add extra Isle style

High waist

Leather bracelets with silver brackets and studs

Skirt and jacket zip together for cohesive look

Remove skirt for lighter, more casual look

Hearts and more hearts!

JEWELED BOOTS

These boots are my favorite to wear. I found each charm and jewel somewhere on the Isle, then hand-painted everything with gold and blue paint.

These aren't perfect, and some of the jewels are chipped—but that adds texture and style. Perfection is boring!

Red iridescent paint for the heart

Gold leather for the crown

Gold studs along the zipper

RED GLOVES

I adore fingerless gloves, unless I'm going for a more formal look.

Red leather for a pop of color

STATEMENT JEWELRY

These were from a broken necklace I found in my mother's closet. I took it apart and used all the pieces.

Red velvet ribbon for the choker

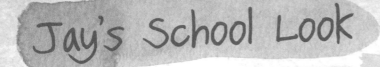

Gold serpent on back of jacket

Hand-dyed blue tank

Bomber jacket with blue leather panels

Cotton drawstring pants
(fabric imported from Never Land)

Jay lives in this jacket I designed for him. I wanted to create something comfortable but cool that he'd love wearing to class. Something that reflects Jay's vibe: relaxed & charming.

Preppy stripes pair perfectly with black fingerless gloves for his Auradon-meets-Isle vibe.

When I design outfits for Jay, I keep in mind how active he is. Even when he's not doing R.O.A.R., he's always moving, always running, or doing pull-ups on whatever bar he can find.

Jay's Isle Look

The knees are reinforced with contrasting blue leather. It looks stylish, but it's also functional. (He's torn two pairs already.)

Yellow and blue jacket trim

Hidden zippers in sleeves

Jacket sleeves are removable, so it transitions through the seasons (or he can take them off if he's working up a sweat.)

Maybe add a cobra on his tank and jacket for a little piece of home (done with a fabric appliqué)

Painted yellow and black leather at collar

Simple black boots—no embellishment

(per Jay's request)

Mal's Green & Gold Dress

Top in sheer fabric with a shell underneath

Green silk to bring out her eyes

Gold and white beading at the neckline

Embroidered gold appliqué for the front piece

Hand-stamped green silk with gold paint, with used gold beading

*Pair with white lace gloves for a more formal look

Gold silk for the trim

GOLD BOOTIES to give it subtle edge
(Mal didn't want me to go too "Isle")

I designed this dress for Mal's meeting with Aladdin and Jasmine. The look is sophisticated and elegant, perfect for high tea or a stroll around Auradon Castle.

This was one of my favorites. Not only was it pretty and on-trend for the occasion, but the flowing fabric made it super comfortable. Mal said she was glad I'd designed the skirt with room to move, since they sat on cushions during dinner.

Mal's Princess Dress

Mal held a press conference in this lovely cap-sleeved dress I designed for her. The cameras at her press conferences can be blinding, and I loved how stunning this looked in the bright lights.

Embroidered lace at collar

Embroidered ribbon at waist
Rectangular sequins sewn on by hand

INVISIBLE HEELS

Clear plastic makes the straps disappear so, the focus is on the gold ornamental dragons.

FIERCE!

(When it was time to make this dress I ended up using a delicate white fabric. The sequins were clear with an iridescent sheen, which brings subtle color to the look.)

♡ ♥ ♡ ♥ ♥ ♡ ♥

WHITE HOT

An all-white look can be achieved with a gorgeous white dress, but also by pairing a white blouse with white jeans or shorts. You can even mix white and cream.

BONUS: try a bright flat or heel for a pop of color.

Inspiration for this dress came when I least expected it. Jane was on the Cotillion planning committee, and they ordered a whole box of these pretty crocheted butterflies, thinking they'd be decorations. Then they realized they couldn't use them. I took them off her hands to create this design for Mal.

Sheer ruffled butterfly sleeves

Pale blue ribbon at waist

Gold and turquoise ribbon trim

Hand-sewn beading

* Embroidered green flowers

Even though Mal ultimately decided the "perfect little lady" look wasn't her thing, I am still glad I got a chance to create so many gorgeous dresses for her. It was a fun challenge to make mischievous Mal look like a proper lady. And I did an amazing job, if I may say so myself.

I know Mal is way more comfortable now in leather and studs (I think it's safe to say all of us VKs are) so I guess I'll be using less lace and satin for her new wardrobe. But maybe she'll need one of these dresses for an event down the road—we can always add an edgy jacket and boots to make her feel more like herself.

Mal's Isle Look

* Emerald green accents to offset the purple pants and jacket

Cut-leather black detailing at the shoulders, creating a "winged" look

Green and purple hand-dyed tank top

Gold and purple bracelets

Hidden zippers in sleeves, for easy removal

SINGLE GLOVE
☆ Pair with a statement ring

Layered chains and belts. I found all different widths, sizes, and colors, and draped them around Mal's hips to add texture.

Gold studs on the jacket and bottom of the pants

Knees reinforced with textured leather

* Asymmetrical seams for that classic Isle style

This was one of my first designs. I hand-sewed every piece and found all the materials from different places on the Isle. The gold chains and studs were in an abandoned warehouse. The purple fabrics I used for the pants were from different jackets I found in an Isle thrift store.

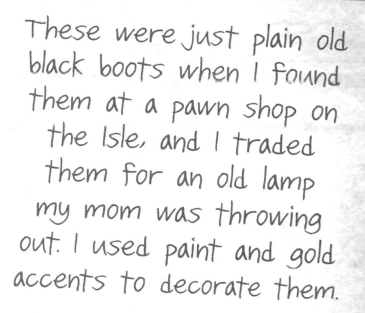

These were just plain old black boots when I found them at a pawn shop on the Isle, and I traded them for an old lamp my mom was throwing out. I used paint and gold accents to decorate them.

STUDDED BOOTS

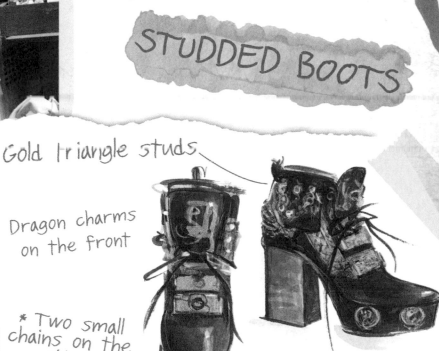

Gold triangle studs

Dragon charms on the front

* Two small chains on the sides

Purple and green paint for the chunky heels

STYLE TIP ♡ ♡ ♡

I love, love, love layering gloves with bracelets. I made bracelets with the remnants from the chains at Mal's waist. Bracelets can be made with almost any type of chain. To add the clasp, you will need a small pair of pliers, plus a lobster clasp and small O-shaped "jump" ring (ask for them at a fabric or bead store).

HOW TO:

1. Open the jump ring with pliers
2. Slide the chain(s) onto the open jump ring
3. Slide the loop at the end of the clasp onto the same open jump ring and close the jump ring

Now you have a bracelet!

ISLE HANDCUFF AND CHAIN RING

Opal stone

Dragon icon

I adore designing jackets that come apart, letting them transition through the seasons. This look can go from fall to winter to spring and then back again.

Transitional items are key for any wardrobe.

MAL'S JACKET— SLEEVELESS

Cropped look

Vests are fun because they come in so many varieties:

Leather = edgy

Embroidered = bohemian

Knit = preppy/cozy

You can wear them with bare arms, with a short-sleeved top underneath, or over a fitted long-sleeved top with a longer coat for a layered look.

Mal wanted something special for her big TV interview, so I designed this dress, making it as "lady of the court" as possible. I would've added a bit more Isle flair to the design, but Mal was clear that she wanted this look to feel as traditionally "Auradon" as possible.

* This length dress is perfect for daytime. To make it less "princessy," swap out heels for some canvas sneakers or espadrilles, and throw a denim jacket over your shoulders.

THE CLUTCH

* Pink satin with pearl beading
* Gold and pearl brooch clasp

Mal's Pretty Pink Dress

Pale pink embroidered lace

Cap sleeve

Pearl beading in white, pink, and gray

Silk ribbon at the waist

White lace gloves create a more formal look

Scalloped hemline

☆ BEADED BRACELETS
Pink rose quartz beads
Gold charms

MAL'S PICNIC DRESS

Halter top with strappy sleeves

Patterned blue silk

* Cutout adds interest to the back

Pale blue ribbons for detailing at the back and waist

Gold brooch at the waist for extra sparkle?

Second ruffle along the middle of the skirt for a super feminine touch

Again, I brought in some edginess with her heels:

Gold booties with embellishment at the ankles

I must've designed a dozen dresses for Mal's dates with Ben, but this is one of my favorites. She wore it to a picnic she planned for him, the same picnic where he discovered she'd been using her spell book in Auradon. . . .

Accessories

Floral brooches ordered from a vendor in Winter's Keep

Thin leather shoulder strap

I found this clear jewelry box at a flea market in Camelot Heights. Instantly, I knew it would make a perfect purse.

Flowered Box Purse

Embroidered flower appliqués with pearl and rhinestone beading

Emerald Hair Clip and Necklace

Emerald brooch imported from Never Land

Gold and emerald dragon pendant

FASHION MUST-HAVES

There are things that <u>feel</u> essential, and then there are ESSENTIALS: the accessories you should always have in your closet because they go with any outfit and can complete any look.

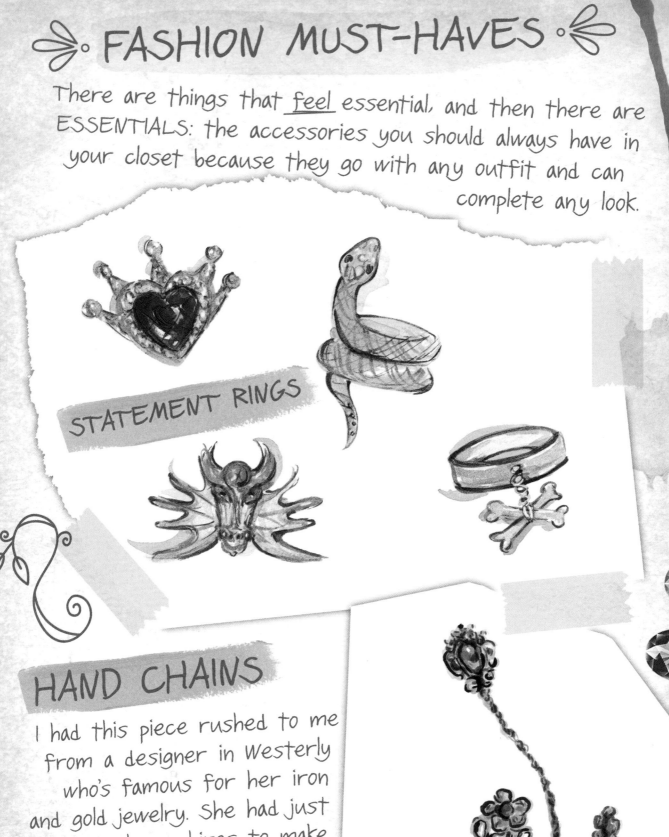

STATEMENT RINGS

HAND CHAINS

I had this piece rushed to me from a designer in Westerly who's famous for her iron and gold jewelry. She had just enough sapphires to make this one-of-a-kind hand chain bracelet and ring to go with Mal's yellow and blue Cotillion dress.

STUDDED
BOOTS

FINGERLESS
GLOVES

BAGS!!!!

Quilted look

Asymmetrical gold zippers

• I cut the broken crown from a sheet of plywood, then spray-painted it gold

Glued-on gold chains and blue jewels for embellishment

Purses, clutches, and backpacks can be great statement pieces. I love to play with color and shape when I'm designing bags for my friends—the more unusual, the better.

*Magic Mirror detail

Gold studs along edge

Gold latches in front

*Poison apple detail

Hand-painted designs in red, yellow, blue, and gold

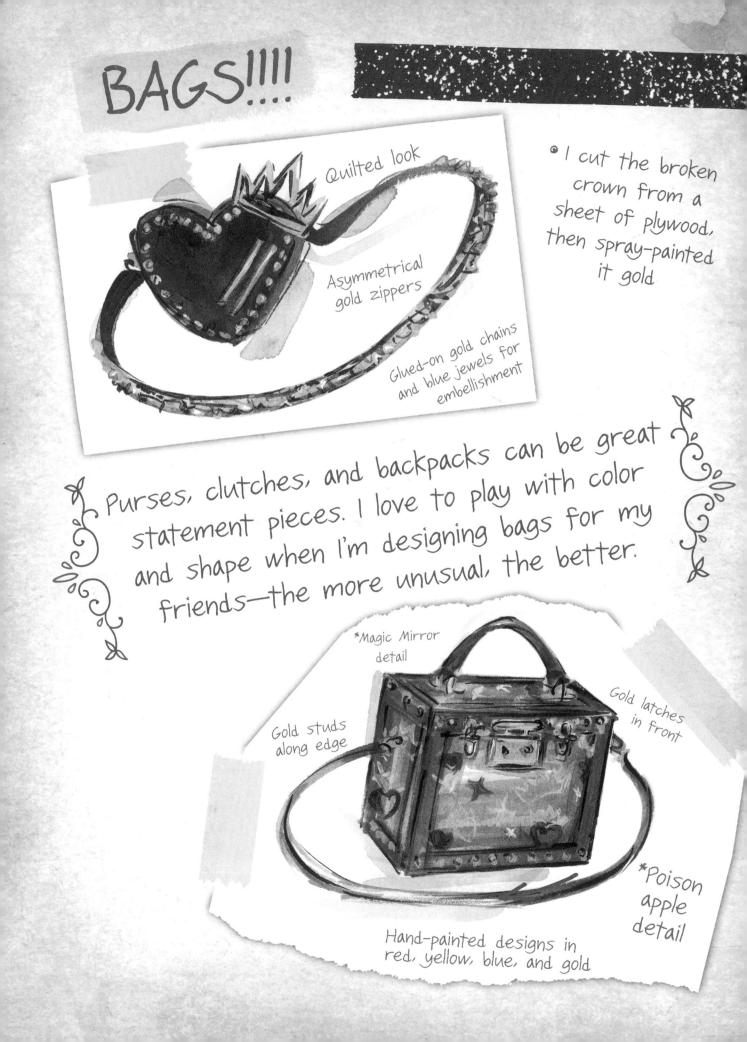

Gold studs along straps and edges

Green and purple embroidered dragon appliqué

Purple and black leather

* Hand-painted with lavender and purple details

Customizing a backpack can be done with pins, paints, or patches. Make your pack represent who you are!

Carlos's School Look

Carlos and I both love wearing red. It's part of our signature styles. I took a risk and put Carlos in a pair of red pants, and thankfully he was into it. Now he calls me his "fashion guru," asking my opinion before he buys anything.

Black and white leather vest

* Hand-painted bones decal on back

Red-and-black wood bead bracelet

☆ Studs on the jacket and bottom of the pants

Red pants with asymmetrical zippers, torn at knees

Carlos is like a little brother to me. I'd do anything for him, and if anyone in Auradon tried to mess with him, they'd have to answer to me. He's one of the kindest, gentlest people I know, which is why it broke my heart to see his heart breaking.

Okay, so maybe it wasn't breaking.
But it was definitely aching.

He had a crush on Jane for so long. I thought about talking to Jane for him, maybe dropping some hints, but I knew he'd be mortified if he found out. So instead, I did what I do best—I styled him in the most confidence-boosting, attention-getting outfits I could design.

(I know I'm biased, but I really think it helped.)

Carlos's Isle Outfit

Accessorize with dog tag necklace

* Red collared shirt layered with ripped white tee

Undone jacket belt creates a casual feel

Fingerless gloves ripped at the knuckles

Red sneaker boots

Jacket Front & Back

Crossed bones detail on back

Zippers at elbows

Painted silver leather for texture

* Red and black leather

If it was up to Carlos, he would only ever wear shorts. The cold doesn't seem to bother him, so I've tried to make that his signature style—layered shorts with boots. I only work with fake fur, and I've made the pieces removable so they can transition through the seasons.

When we went back to the Isle, it was kind of crazy. As soon as I stepped out of the limo, all the memories flooded back. We passed the pawn shop where I traded my broken speakers for an old sewing machine. There was the street vendor who I always bought brine-flavored chips from. One of the shops I'd loved, this little place that sold used clothing, had closed since I left.

I'm definitely happier living in Auradon, but I'd kind of forgotten there are things I still love about the Isle. That there is hidden beauty everywhere. How it'll always be a part of me. I want to incorporate more Isle into my designs—I'm even thinking of pulling inspiration from Uma's and Harry's looks . . .

WELCOME TO THE ISLE

SCALLYWAG SWAG

Incorporating Pirate Style into Your Wardrobe

Uma's Isle Style

Tarnished pins and brooches for hat and lapel

*Leather fringes at shoulders

– Hand-painted skull on tank

– Purple mesh sleeves with ripped black netting

– Purple mesh at neckline

Cropped jacket

* Painted leather gives the look a tie-dye feel

Even if she kidnapped Ben and almost made him shark bait, I can't deny that Uma has one-of-a-kind style. Since I've been back, I've pulled inspiration from her look for some of my latest designs.

Leather fringes on skirt
Metallic netting for skirt

* Multiple thick belts in different colors

* On the Isle, people paint leather to hide excessive wear. It's also great for adding dimension to an otherwise ordinary jacket or vest.

Gold skull buckle adds edge

• Rips and tears add immediate grittiness.

(I used this to add texture to my T-shirt and Carlos's red pants.)

BIG RINGS

Scarves as scarve OR as belts

• Feathers in hats
  (or in clips/hairpieces,

○ Add leather and brass

• Braided belts

• Gold skull charms

○ Nautical details

• Wharf netting layered
  into jackets and
  scarves

Just a few ideas I came up with . . .

Pirate-Style Hats

MORE PIRATE-STYLE DESIGNS

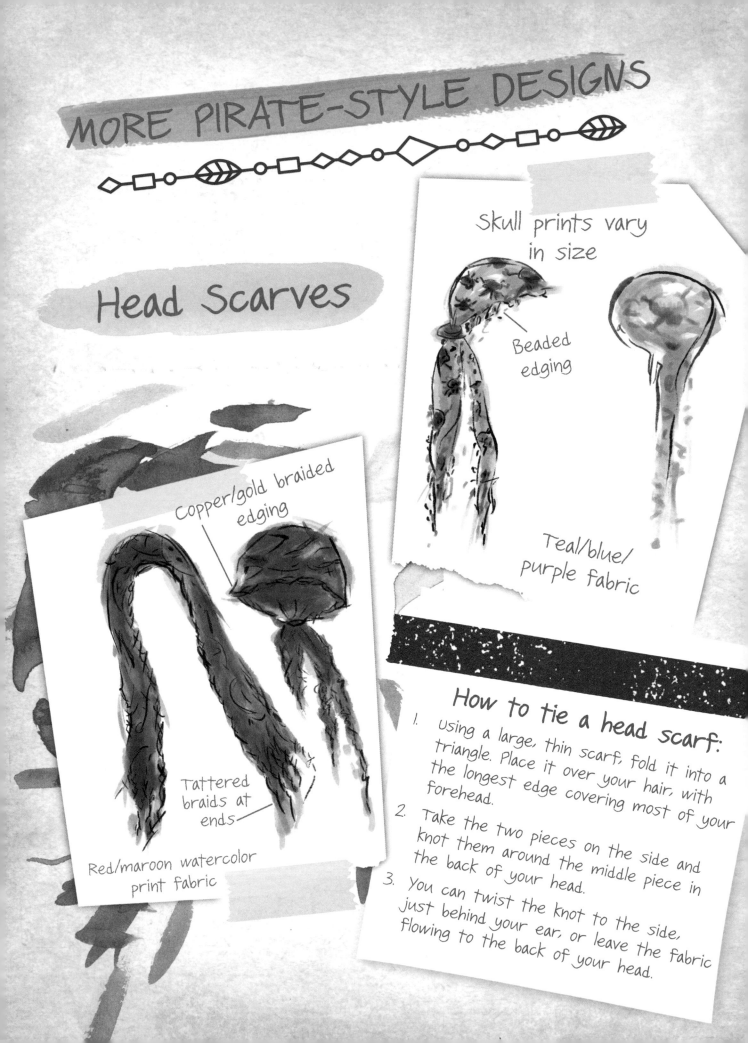

Head Scarves

Skull prints vary in size

Beaded edging

Teal/blue/ purple fabric

Copper/gold braided edging

Tattered braids at ends

Red/maroon watercolor print fabric

How to tie a head scarf:

1. Using a large, thin scarf, fold it into a triangle. Place it over your hair, with the longest edge covering most of your forehead.

2. Take the two pieces on the side and knot them around the middle piece in the back of your head.

3. You can twist the knot to the side, just behind your ear, or leave the fabric flowing to the back of your head.

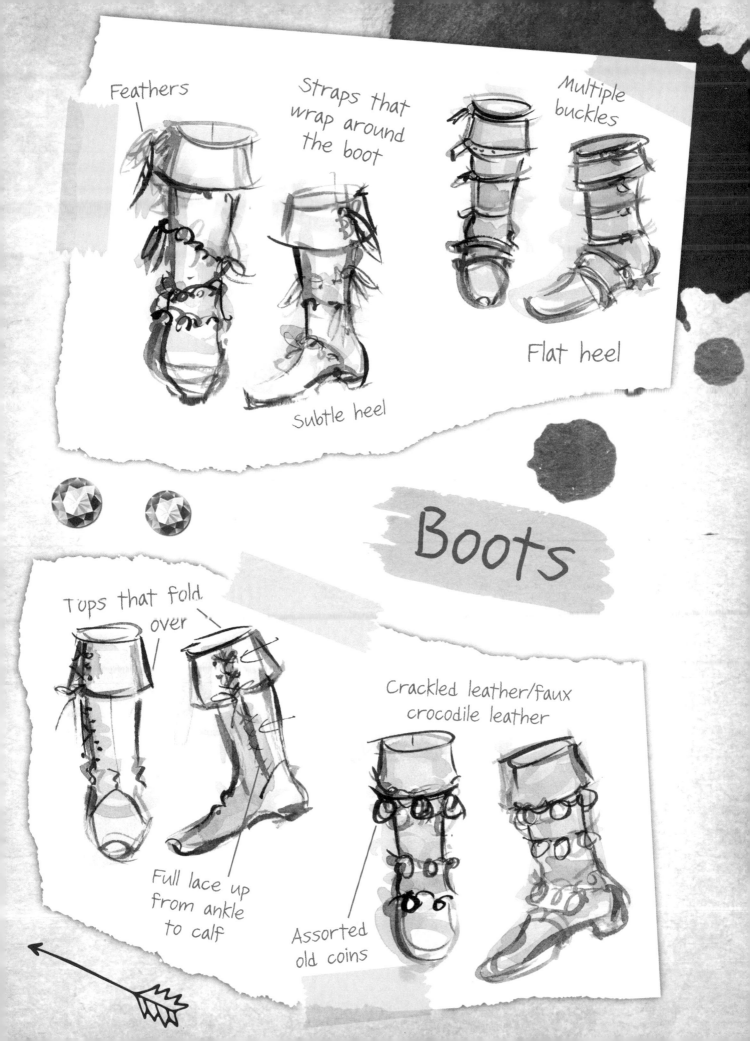

Feathers

Straps that wrap around the boot

Multiple buckles

Subtle heel

Flat heel

Boots

Tops that fold over

Crackled leather/faux crocodile leather

Full lace up from ankle to calf

Assorted old coins

Sweet / Ruffled

SHIRTS

Sophisticated victorian pirate

Classic crisp white cotton

Laces up sides

Peplum "skirt"

Full lace-up

Pearl eyes

White Gold

Chain ring

Rubies, rubies, rubies!

Rings

Paint on sterling Silver (using nailpolish?)

Dizzy is one of my favorite people in the entire world. It's not often that you find someone so sweet and talented, with her own unique perspective on everything. Even though Dizzy hasn't come to Auradon (yet), I can still picture her as if she's standing right in front of me. I love how creative and playful she was in designing her own special look.

Dizzy's Isle Style

Signature headphones

Emerald
blouse
with poufy
sleeves

Brooch in center
of collar, a
twist on Lady
Tremaine's look

* Apron for
function, but
adds a layer of
interest

Emerald green
splattered tulle
for fullness in
the skirt

Paint splattered everything!

The first time I met Dizzy was because I happened to ask a random girl on the street—who had a fierce haircut—who her stylist was.
She told me "Dizzy" and slipped me the address, and I immediately ran off to find her.

When I walked into Dizzy's place on the other side of town, I was shocked. I was expecting some woman my mom's age, and instead there was a girl in a paint-spattered apron. She was younger than I was, and she was doing hair out of her bedroom—she just had a bucket and an old rusty pair of scissors and this broken chair she made her clients sit in. But it didn't matter. She had the most important thing: she had vision.

Once I sat in that broken chair, we just connected. We started sharing details about our lives with each other. Our hopes and our dreams. The things we loved and the things we were most afraid of. (Dizzy is terrified of the number thirteen and snakes.)

Auradon, Dizzy's grandmother, Lady Tremaine, heard about what Dizzy had been doing. She wasn't happy about it, so she axed Dizzy's side business and put her to work sweeping floors in her shop, making her swear not to cut hair on her own.

That's where I found her when I went back to the Isle—in Lady Tremaine's Curl Up and Dye. She's still as creative as ever, and she started designing hairpieces out of different odds and ends. She's been using old keys, lace, and parts from a broken watch to make headbands. They're all so unique and beautiful. She gave me a whole bunch to bring back to Auradon with me. She said it made her happy to know at least a part of her would make it there. . . .

Walking out of that salon and leaving Dizzy behind . . . I think that's one of the hardest things I've ever had to do. She deserves the same opportunities that I have in Auradon. She deserves to shine, and for everyone to see how unique and special she is. She deserves a chance. I'm glad she's going to get one!

DIZZY'S STYLE:
GLASSES AND APRONS

I just think her style is so cute and SO HER! I designed a few more pairs of glasses that were inspired by the ones she wears, plus some apron-front dresses.

How to:

Even if you have perfect vision, you can still get glasses!

⭐ Source your local thrift store for frames without lenses—I call these "fashion specs"!

⭐ You can also look there for aprons.

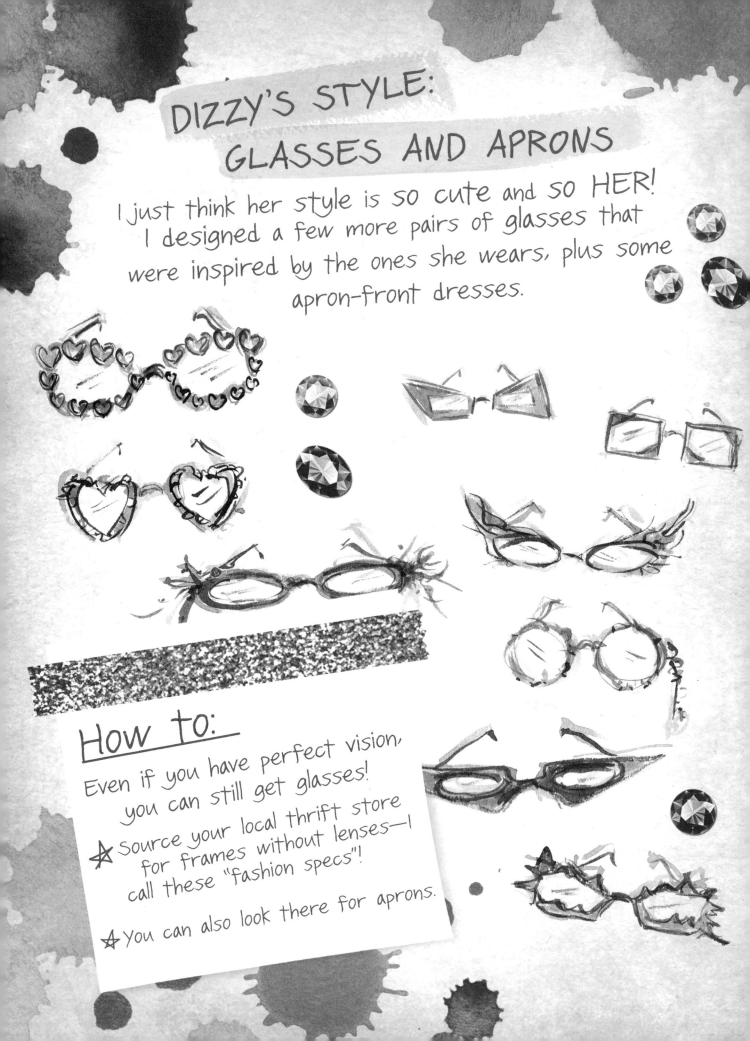

ISLE INSPIRATION

Going back to the Isle, I was reminded of all the hidden beauty that place holds. Sure, it doesn't look anything like the clean, cobbled streets of Auradon, but there's always something interesting to look at (and spaces and objects I've never seen anywhere else). I have to figure out how to incorporate some of its beauty into my next designs. . . .

The Isle streets have these colorful lanterns I love. The color pops against a drab backdrop.

When you only have junkyard scraps to work with, you have to get creative. On the Isle it's common to see panes of glass painted over—paint can make dingy things come to life!

Signs hand-written on pieces of rotted wood or old scraps remind me how cool repurposed items can be.

Dizzy's apron is always covered with paint. Paint spatter adds texture and color to plain fabrics or accessories.

The Isle was a tough place to grow up.

I'm not saying what Uma did at Cotillion was right. I know better than that. But part of me can understand where she's coming from. Mal, Jay, Carlos, and I have all gotten opportunities that no other villain kids have. We attend dances and parties, high teas, and R.O.A.R. games. We're in one of the best schools and we're learning more than we could anywhere else. Maybe what made Uma the angriest was that we left the Isle and didn't look back.

I keep seeing that little kid's face—the one on the Isle who tried to steal just a few coins from me. That kid wasn't so different from who I was just a year ago when I lived there. I can't stop thinking about Dizzy in her grandmother's shop. It's such a waste that she's there sweeping floors when we could all use her talent here.

After Cotillion was over, Ben promised that if I made a list of Isle kids who should come to Auradon, he'd help me bring them over. I'll be in charge of selecting the kids based on their desire and need.

Headphones

Dizzy wears these around her neck, like a backwards necklace. It's easy for her to pop them on when she wants to listen to music, and they're so pretty that your eye is drawn to them, framing the antique brooch in the center of her collar.

≫ I designed these for me and my friends: ≪

Tiara-like accent on top —

MY HEADPHONES

—Soft red ear pads

Signature heart + gemstones

The months leading up to Cotillion were madness.

I'd get shipment after shipment of supplies in, and Doug and I would scramble to sort through them. I'd stay up late hand-sewing sequins onto skirts or calling vendors in Camelot Heights, trying to find the perfect bracelet for Jane. Doug was so sweet and supportive through all of it. He even helped me when I needed an extra set of hands (but I always had to check to make sure his stitches were straight).

So I barely had time to process what a big deal Cotillion would be for Evie's 4 Hearts. It wasn't until we walked onto the yacht that I realized how much my hard work had paid off. So many people came up to me, complimenting me on my designs.

I saw Lonnie in her coral silk gown. Jane's big pink bow looked perfect where I'd sewn it on her waist, giving the dress an eye-catching detail. All the girls who were wearing Evie's 4 Hearts eventually made their way over to me, telling me how much they loved their gowns. But maybe the best moment was when Lumiere announced Mal and she strode down the stairs in her new VK-inspired dress. She looked like my best friend again. Her hair was back to its radiant purple, and I'd paired her gown with boots and leather bracelets, giving it an edgy look.

Already I'm thinking about Auradon Prep's next big event and all the designs I could make in the coming months. Sometimes I'll pass Jane in the hall and imagine another evening gown for her, something in fuchsia or carnation pink. I'm already designing another school dress for Lonnie.

TRENDS FROM AURADON PREP'S COTILLION

BRIGHT COLORS MAKE BOLD STATEMENTS.

OMG!

<u>Designer (Evie)</u> showed off her versatility last night with a variety of hot new looks. Here's what we learned from the red carpet.

GOLD SANDALS

BROOCHES AND BOWS ARE IN.

Cotillion Hair and Makeup

A bold eyebrow looked amazing on Lonnie, because the rest of her makeup was minimal.

And coral eyeshadow paired beautifully with her dress.

When it came to Lonnie's hair we decided to do half-up/half-down, and to crimp the length of it for added texture.

I did my chignon with a side-part, and then pulled out a tendril in front to curl. And the hair accessory was the final touch.

I did my normal makeup which is black mascara blue shadow, and a rosy lip, just amped it up a bit for a nighttime look.

Mal's purple hair is the real star here. It brings out her green eyes.

I love the way her eyeliner wings out a bit in the corners—it draws attention to her green eyes. That, and a little rose-colored blush, were perfect for all the photos she took at Cotillion.

Jane's makeup is simple and clean. Nude lipstick, peachy eye shadow, and a lengthening mascara. Perfection.

She wore her hair down and those long dark tresses looked beautiful against the blue of her dress.

Jane planned Cotillion, so she wanted to stand out as the hostess with the most.

NAME: _Jane_

I'M IN THE MARKET FOR (CHECK ALL THAT APPLY):

☑ EVENING GOWN
☐ PARTY DRESS
☐ PANTS
☐ JACKET
☐ BLOUSE
☑ PURSE
☐ BACKPACK

☑ JEWELRY — Pair with a necklace
+ Add bracelets to gloves
☑ GLOVES
☐ BOOTS
☑ HEELS
☐ HAT
☐ SCARF

Jane is the girliest of girls. Loves pastels and florals. Feels most comfortable in outfits with super feminine touches, like bows and lace.

MY STYLE IS: _Classic. I love big skirts and bows. Think Bibbidi-Bobbidi-Boo but more modern._

SIGNATURE COLORS: _Pastels. Sky blue, carnation pink, and lavender._

MATERIALS THAT MAKE ME SWOON: _Silk and chiffon_ Likes polka dots, too, and lace!

I NEED THIS FOR: _The biggest event of the year . . . Cotillion!_

DREAM FASHION SCENARIO: _Ummm, doing something more exciting than serving punch in this dress._

DESCRIBE YOUR PERSONALITY IN A WORD OR TWO: _Thoughtful_

AVAILABLE FOR FITTINGS?: _Yes. I just have to make sure nothing conflicts with my duties for the Cotillion planning committee._

* Jane is slowly developing more of her own style. When I first met her, she was really shy and hesitant to make any big fashion decisions on her own. I wanted to elevate her look and have her red carpet Cotillion walk officially announce her as a fashion force to be reckoned with!

Behind the Scenes of Auradon's Cotillion

"I LOVED COLLABORATING WITH MAL ON ALL THE DETAILS FOR COTILLION. SHE WAS EASY TO WORK WITH AND HAD INPUT ON EVERYTHING FROM FLOWER ARRANGEMENTS TO PARTY FAVORS. I'M LOOKING FORWARD TO WORKING WITH OUR NEW LADY OF THE COURT AGAIN."

The Auradon Prep Cotillion is an event for the ages. Every year the ball seems to be more impressive than the year before. We followed Jane, head of the Cotillion planning committee, in the week leading up to this year's big night.

Jane knew she wanted to make the venue unique. "Of course a yacht is a special place to hold a Cotillion, but this yacht party needed to be extraordinary," Jane said. "I wanted all of the decorations to really make the ball feel like its own special world, far away from the rest of Auradon." She figured that the *True Love* yacht shouldn't just be docked in the harbor and decided it would cruise around the coast as Auradon's finest danced into the night.

Continued on page 11

JANE'S COTILLION LOOK

Tulle butterfly sleeves

Tiny rhinestones for sparkle

Silk fuchsia bow, turned to the side to create a fun, playful feel

White bow bracelet

Pale blue layered tulle skirt

* Converts into shorter frock for when dancing kicks into high gear!

Bracelets and Bow Accessories

Gold chain bracelet threaded with lavender ribbon

GET THE LOOK: Tie a long thin scarf into a bow around your waist, like a belt. Or take a simple piece of black velvet ribbon (about the length of your arm) and make a bow necklace to wear against a white tank or tee.

(Bow should tie just below your collarbone.)

Clasp made from an antique brooch from the Summerlands
(two in the set, one used for ring)

* Gold clasp bracelet with purple rhinestone bows

A bow is SUPER chic!

This was one of the more time-consuming purses I've made. It took days to get all the beading right, but it couldn't have been more perfect with Jane's gown.

* Blue rhinestone beading

* Gold and diamond pendants from a broken necklace

JEWELED CLUTCH

J

Dear Evie,

Thank you so much for designing my gown for Cotillion (and so many of the beautiful dresses I wear to school). All the details were perfect—from the big pink silk bow to the rhinestone heels that glittered with each step I took. It was even better than what I imagined, and I loved hosting the party in it (even when things got a little crazy). I'm lucky to call such a talented, kind person my friend.

With love,
Jane ♡

Carlos finally ended up asking Jane to Cotillion at the last minute, which didn't give me much time to coordinate their outfits. Red and black doesn't pair perfectly with pale blue and pink, but there are subtle touches that might've made the looks complement one another. Like a corsage, for example—I designed one that Carlos could give Jane (maybe he will at the next big event. . .)

They make an adorable couple
(even when they're soaked in sea water).

Carlos wasn't completely convinced he should wear a jacket, and he initially would've rather gone with something a little less formal. I insisted, though, and he was glad I did—everyone at Cotillion was super dressed up.

The short pants were perfect for Carlos. He said they were made for dancing the whole night. I love when my designs are functional as well as fashionable!

Crisp white
button-down
underneath

Embroidered
gold appliqué on
front panel

Gold medallion
and chain

Cropped
Jacket

*Cropped
above
waist

* Gold buttons

Black and
white panels
for color block
effect

— Red
fingerless
gloves

Red cotton
shorts with
leather panels

This jacket
is formal
without being
too formal.
Inspired by
my red
leather jacket,
I wanted
to make
Carlos
a piece that
felt uniquely
him—that mix
of Auradon
and Isle style.

Asymmetrical
black zippers

Black socks
peeking
over boots

I'm already trying to figure out where I can wear this gown again. Yes, I know it's supposed to be for Cotillion, and too special to wear anywhere else, but I can't bear to think of it just wasting away in my closet.

* Gold crown embellishments

One strap
+ Braided strap with silver embellishment

*Royal blue ribbon at waist

Gold and ruby crown bracelet

* Paired with a gold and ruby statement ring

Long Polished Red Leather Gloves

Mermaid train

*Royal blue silk with blue and silver beading

MY FAVORITE GOWN

Beaded sapphire and pearl bracelets

I took my usual fingerless gloves to the next level by adding sleeves to the elbow. The seam is on the front, creating subtle ruching.

Special Occasion Jewelry

Normally, I make my own jewelry, but I decided to splurge on these pieces from a jeweler in Belle's Harbor. I designed these but had the jeweler make them. I used some of the money I made with my business, so whenever I look at them I'll remember what it was like just starting out in Auradon.

Be Mine

* Gold choker necklace with diamonds

Gold
crown
earrings

Doug's Gold and Black Suit

GOLD SATIN

Black satin lapel and bow tie

Black satin trim for pockets

Black patent leather shoes

I knew Doug and I were going to Cotillion together before I designed a single outfit. Originally, I thought I'd put him in a red and blue suit, but Doug has always had his own unique style and I wanted to honor that. Since gold and black go with blue, we still looked great standing next to each other.

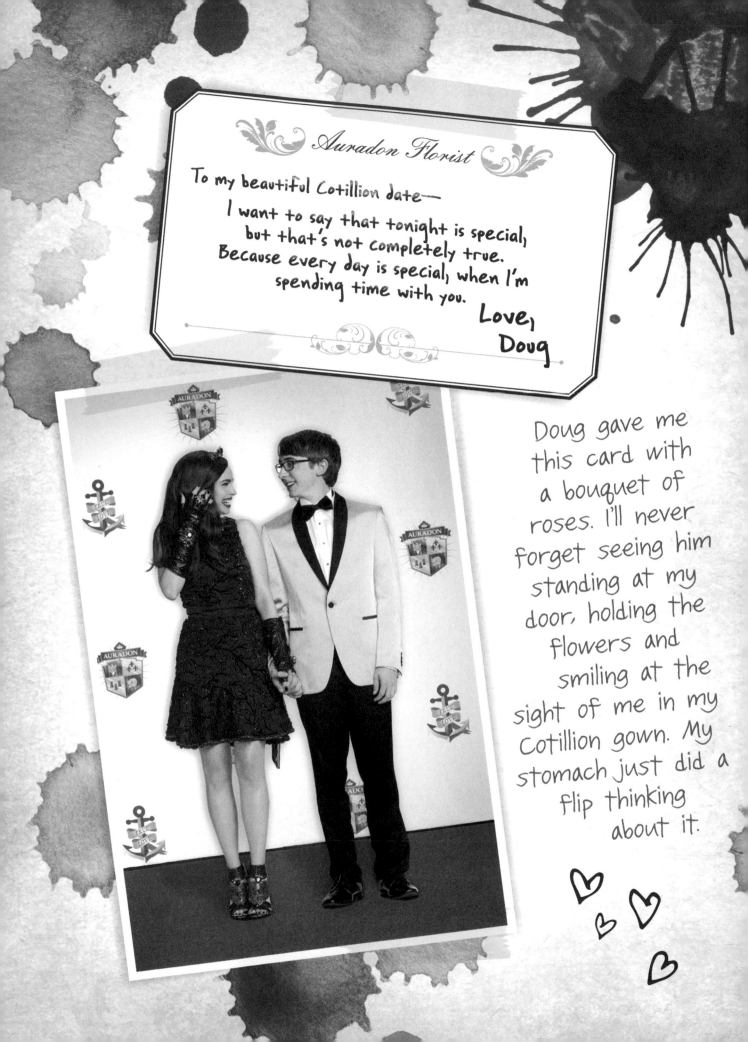

Auradon Florist

To my beautiful Cotillion date—

I want to say that tonight is special, but that's not completely true. Because every day is special, when I'm spending time with you.

Love,
Doug

Doug gave me this card with a bouquet of roses. I'll never forget seeing him standing at my door, holding the flowers and smiling at the sight of me in my Cotillion gown. My stomach just did a flip thinking about it.

I've never seen a more spectacular sight than the *True Love* yacht docked in the harbor, glittering in the moonlight.

All of Jane's and Mal's Cotillion planning was worth it. Sparkling lights crisscrossed the deck, colorful centerpieces decorated every table, and the DJ played music that made everyone want to dance. As Doug and I walked in, dozens of cameras flashed in our direction. People shouted questions about the headpieces, or wanted details about designs.

Of course, Cotillion didn't go exactly as planned. But Doug was by my side the whole time, even through the scary parts. Afterwards we danced for hours. Doug started this dance move that caught on with the rest of the guests, and soon everyone was doing it. My face hurt from smiling so much.

It's just . . . it means so much having someone who loves me for who I am. Doug loves the chemistry nerd in me, and the popular designer in me, and the part of me that panics when thirty boxes of fabric show up at my door. If this isn't true love, I can't imagine what is.

Uma's Cotillion Look

Okay, so maybe Uma, daughter of Ursula and party crasher extraordinaire, shouldn't be in this book, but I couldn't resist. Because the truth (even if Auradon kids don't want to admit it) is that Uma has impeccable taste. I've admired her style for years, even if I never really admired her as a person.

Tarnished gold pins on shoulders

* Turquoise lace at neckline

Pale blue and turquoise sequins

SHELL NECKLACE

This is an iconic piece of jewelry, with so much history. It is also really pretty and makes me think about incorporating more shells and beach-inspired charms into my designs. After all, I am from an island. . . .

Polished brown leather gloves

Gold and silver netting folded into skirt
+
Embroidered gold and turquoise silk pieces i skirt

* Skirt layered with different silks and colored tulle

CLUTCHES

If I'd been consulting with Uma for the Cotillion, I would've suggested she go with a small silver or gold embellished clutch, shaped like a seashell. I designed these just for fun.

- Starfish clasp imported from a vendor in the Summerlands
- Gold and rhinestone flecked
- Turquoise beading

view from side, opens like a real shell

wrist chain strap

Dizzy's Hair Accessories

These one-of-a-kind hair accessories Dizzy made are incredible. I'm blown away by the subtle detail in each one. There are beads and flowers, tassels and braids. I can't wait to see what she creates next.

Heart rhinestones

Simple gold crown comb

I kept this one for myself and wore it to Cotillion. . . . Can you blame me?

Repurposed gold chain

Pigeon feathers, dyed purple

* Found gemstones
and rose charms

Yellow flower made from netting,
wire, and beads

Tassel
made from
pink strips
of sponge

Gold leaves flecked
with turquoise paint

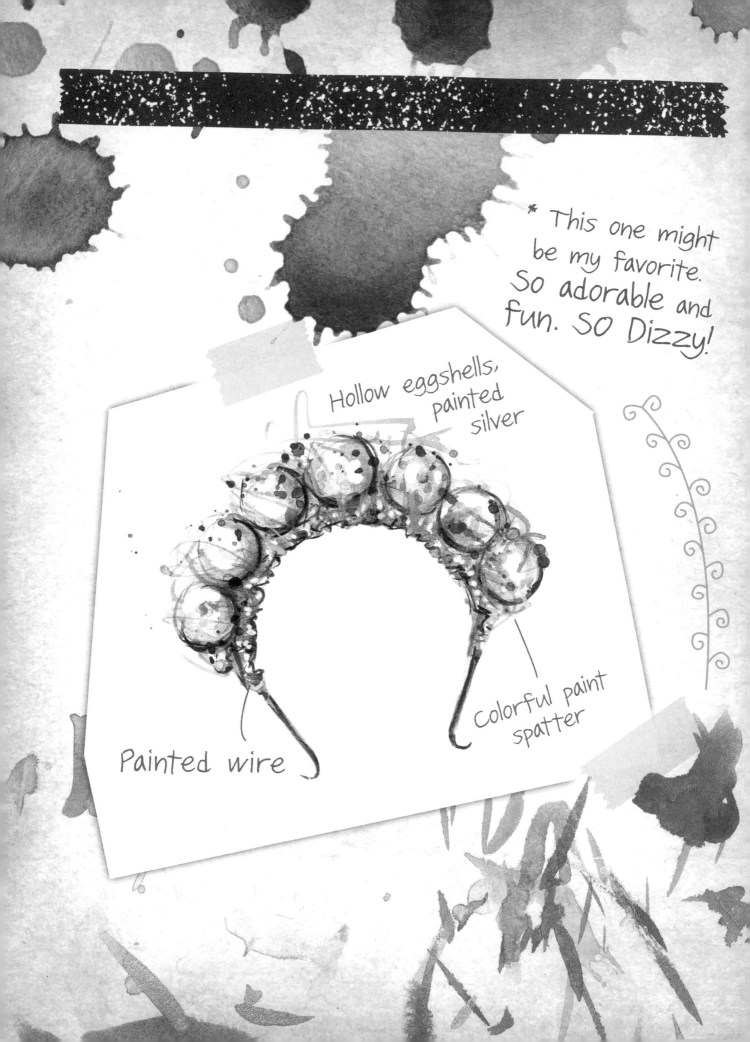

* This one might be my favorite. So adorable and fun. SO Dizzy!

Hollow eggshells, painted silver

Colorful paint spatter

Painted wire

Recycled watch chain

Papier-mâche bow,
painted gold

Old brooches

— I think Jane will absolutely love this one.
It's the perfect accessory to bring a little
"Isle style" to her look!

The press at Cotillion wanted to know about the hair accessories and how I'd come up with them. So of course I was so excited when I told them "the hair accessories tonight are by Dizzy of the Isle!" And all the reporters scribbled down her name as they tried to figure out who this new designer was. I smiled, imagining Dizzy watching on TV from Lady Tremaine's shop. Maybe she saw how excited everyone was about her accessories (at least I hope she did).

I was given an opportunity to come to Auradon, and I want to make sure Dizzy has similar opportunities in the future. I already have a plan for what's next for her. Since Cotillion, my phone has been ringing nonstop and there have been dozens of reporters calling me about Dizzy, but I haven't answered a single one. Because when she gets here I want her to be the one giving interviews and having her photo taken. She deserves it.

GO DIZZY!!!....

Who is "DIZZY OF THE ISLE"?

The Story Behind Auradon's New Accessories Designer

At last night's Cotillion, the world was introduced to fashion hair accessories. These one-of-a-kind items are made with found objects like keys, watch parts, and rusted gears. They come in the form of clips, combs, and headbands. Each accessory is a small but intricate piece of art, like the one worn by Evie, Auradon Prep's resident fashionista, in the photo below.

When asked about her latest creations, Evie was quick to give credit to a mysterious new designer. "These are by Dizzy of the Isle!" she announced to the crowd. But Evie disappeared into the yacht before we could get further information. At the time of publication, we still hadn't heard back from her for further comment.

When I was designing Jay's outfit for Cotillion, I kept reminding myself that I was introducing Auradon to a new kind of hero, one they'd never met before. Jay is fierce and funny, and maybe even a little bit scary (I blame his dad for that), but inside he is all sweetness. I wanted everyone to see this true gentleman from the Isle.

* Olive branch gold-embroidered appliqué on back—a reminder that Auradon and the Isle are no longer enemies

Chain embellishment on shoulder

Gold embroidered appliqués on sleeves

Buttons on front reminiscent of Prince Eric's wedding coat

Red and blue polished leather

Tan suede pants

Jacket has tails, for a more regal look

NAME: __Lonnie__

I'M IN THE MARKET FOR (CHECK ALL THAT APPLY):

- ☑ EVENING GOWN
- ☐ PARTY DRESS
- ☐ PANTS
- ☐ JACKET
- ☐ BLOUSE
- ☑ PURSE
- ☐ BACKPACK

- ☐ JEWELRY
- ☐ GLOVES
- ☐ BOOTS
- ☑ HEELS
- ☐ HAT
- ☐ SCARF

MY STYLE IS: __Elegant but comfortable. I love my mom's style— I've drawn a lot of inspiration from her closet.__

SIGNATURE COLORS: __Fuchsia and turquoise. Do I really have to wear other colors?__

MATERIALS THAT MAKE ME SWOON: __Silk. It's so soft.__

I NEED THIS FOR: __Cotillion__

DREAM FASHION SCENARIO: __A super fancy gown that lets me be active!__

DESCRIBE YOUR PERSONALITY IN A WORD OR TWO: __Fierce!__

AVAILABLE FOR FITTINGS?: __Whenever you need me!__

Lonnie loves fuchsia
and turquoise, but I wanted to
do something a little more special for
her Cotillion dress. I played with different
color palettes revolving around a warm
printed coral silk. And I gave her pants
instead of a skirt—I knew she would
love that!

I made all the dresses so that they could transition from long and formal to dance party ready.

TRY IT :

GOLD SHOES

Gold leather heels, flats, or sandals are great because gold is a universal color—you can pair it with almost any shade or pattern of clothing.

Gold gladiator heel

Rhinestone embellishment

Lonnie's Cotillion Look

Black, fuchsia, and turquoise train down the back + sheer panel in back

*Sheer halter top with shell underneath

— Lavender ribbon at neckline

*Keyhole in front

Turquoise ribbon at the waist and sleeves

High-waisted pants

Printed coral silk for skirt and pants

Sheer tulle to add fullness to skirt

They all look so GOOD! Seeing them together like this is incredible!

COTILLION'S

The gentlemen of Auradon Prep stepped out last night, looking fabulous in Evie's 4 Hearts suits.

KING BEN

JAY

BEST-DRESSED

CARLOS

DOUG

Chad's Cotillion Look

Gold chain at front
+
Gold piping on collar

* Medals—I don't know what Chad got these for, but he insisted I put them on there

*Gold accents at shoulders

Gold embroidered appliqués for sleeves and front panel

Gold and royal blue silk trim on sleeves and front

Chad. Prince Charming's son, and the most difficult customer I've ever had. We managed to find common ground with this classic baby-blue suit. I was inspired by the Auradon princes of long ago and their proper, preppy style.

The Cape
- Royal blue velvet
- Fake hyena fur

This was the most fun part of designing Chad's outfit (and it wasn't that fun). I managed to get him to agree to the fake fur trim, and it really elevated his style. He didn't make it to Cotillion, but maybe he'll wear it to the next formal event. . . .

Chad fought me on everything. He kept changing his mind, saying he wanted a cape one week and then deciding he hated it the next. It made me feel a bit like I was losing my mind . . . Was my memory not working right?

AURADON

Evie—

I've been thinking about your design for my Cotillion outfit, and we need to make some last-minute alterations. I know Cotillion is only a day away, but please make these changes as soon as possible.

1.   Should we do silver buttons instead of gold?
                              Just a thought.
2.   Let's do fake lion mane instead of hyena fur—it's just too much. I don't want people laughing at me.
3.   I'm questioning the pale blue fabric. Maybe we go with a gold suit instead? My father loves gold— it's a family color.
4.   Don't think the cape should be velvet.
5.   Too many gold embroidered thingies.
6.   Pants should be tighter.
7.   Maybe we should do silver buttons.
          Yes, silver buttons it is!

Thanks! you're the best!

Chad

Ben's Cotillion Outfit

Gold tassels, reminiscent of Prince Charming's jacket

* Gold piping on collar, reminiscent of Beast's jacket

Embroidered gold ribbon at collar

* Gold embroidered appliqué on front panel

Royal blue leather at the cuffs

Royal blue satin jacket

* Gold beast belt buckle

Royal blue leather panels in pants

All eyes were on Ben and Mal at Cotillion, so I knew I had to deliver with their designs. Ben is coming into his own as king, and I wanted all of Auradon to not just see him as Beast's son, but also as a new leader worthy of respect.

- Family medals
  - Embroidered family crest
  - Gold olive branch appliqué, reminding us of unity

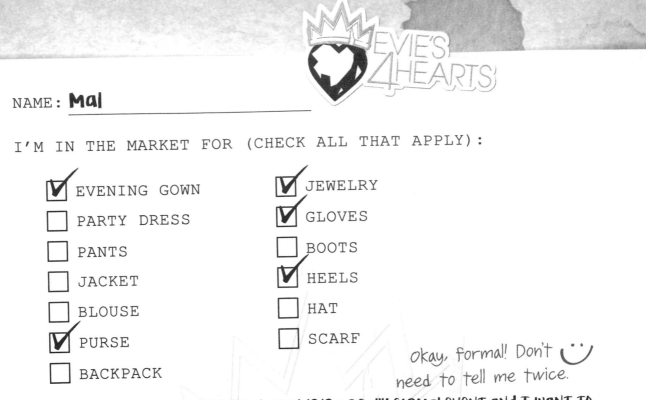

NAME: **Mal**

I'M IN THE MARKET FOR (CHECK ALL THAT APPLY):

☑ EVENING GOWN   ☑ JEWELRY
☐ PARTY DRESS   ☑ GLOVES
☐ PANTS   ☐ BOOTS
☐ JACKET   ☑ HEELS
☐ BLOUSE   ☐ HAT
☑ PURSE   ☐ SCARF
☐ BACKPACK

Okay, formal! Don't ☺ need to tell me twice.

MY STYLE IS: Normally edgy, but this is a really formal event and I want to make sure I look like a true Auradon lady. I want to look poised and pulled together, like all the princesses and ladies that we read about in Auradon textbooks.

SIGNATURE COLORS: Purple. But lately it doesn't feel like it's appropriate...So I guess I could live without it. And maybe I should.

MATERIALS THAT MAKE ME SWOON: I used to really love python pleather, but ✓ again, that wouldn't be appropriate. How about silk and tulle? ✓

I NEED THIS FOR: Cotillion. It will be very formal. I'll be introduced to everyone as lady of the court. I need to look prim and proper, beautiful and polished, and like someone the people of Auradon can look up to. So basically this outfit needs to be perfect, Evie. NO PRESSURE!

DREAM FASHION SCENARIO: I show up and everyone thinks I look worthy of being lady of the court.

DESCRIBE YOUR PERSONALITY IN A WORD OR TWO: Still wicked...BUT TRYING TO BE PROPER.

AVAILABLE FOR FITTINGS?: Evie. I'm your roommate. Duh.

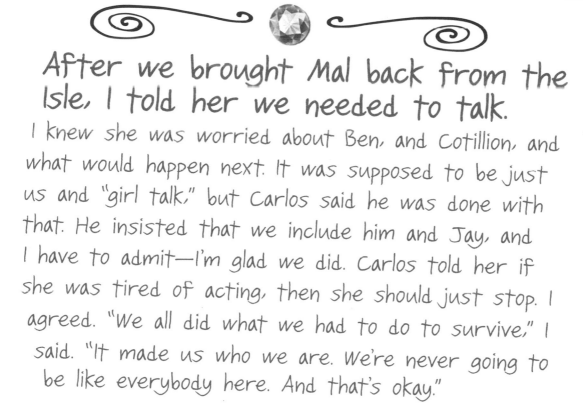

After we brought Mal back from the Isle, I told her we needed to talk.

I knew she was worried about Ben, and Cotillion, and what would happen next. It was supposed to be just us and "girl talk," but Carlos said he was done with that. He insisted that we include him and Jay, and I have to admit—I'm glad we did. Carlos told her if she was tired of acting, then she should just stop. I agreed. "We all did what we had to do to survive," I said. "It made us who we are. We're never going to be like everybody here. And that's okay."

As I said it, I knew it was true for me, too. I'd tried so hard to forget what happened on the Isle, who I used to be. But it's those experiences that made me who I am. And I like that I'm different. It's why my designs are so unique. It's why no one else has the same hairstyle I do, or why no one is ever wearing the same boots as me or the same backpack. I'm 100 percent Evie. Totally original. I wanted to make Mal feel the same way. That's why I made all those last-minute changes to her Cotillion gown, bringing in that VK edge that I knew, deep down, she loved.

Mal's Cotillion Gown

Blue embroidered accent along collar

Tiny rhinestones for sparkle

Royal blue soft tulle for the train
+
Royal blue beading and lace

Blue and yellow tulle for a wide, full skirt

After everything went down, I had to design this Cotillion gown to make it more HER. I wanted it to combine her new and old looks and show that she could stay true to who she is and still look amazing as Auradon royalty.

Mesh Boots

I am obsessed with these boots I created for her new Cotillion look. I spent hours gluing on those tiny rhinestones and gold studs, but it was totally worth it.

- Yellow leather boots with yellow felt piping
- Blue embroidered appliqué

Hidden zipper in back

Lucite heel covered in gold studs

Pointy toe

☆ Extra studs around leg opening = extra edgy

* I added all these tiny rhinestones for extra sparkle

CLUTCH PURSE

* This had a lot of metalworked design. It was heavy but looked awesome.

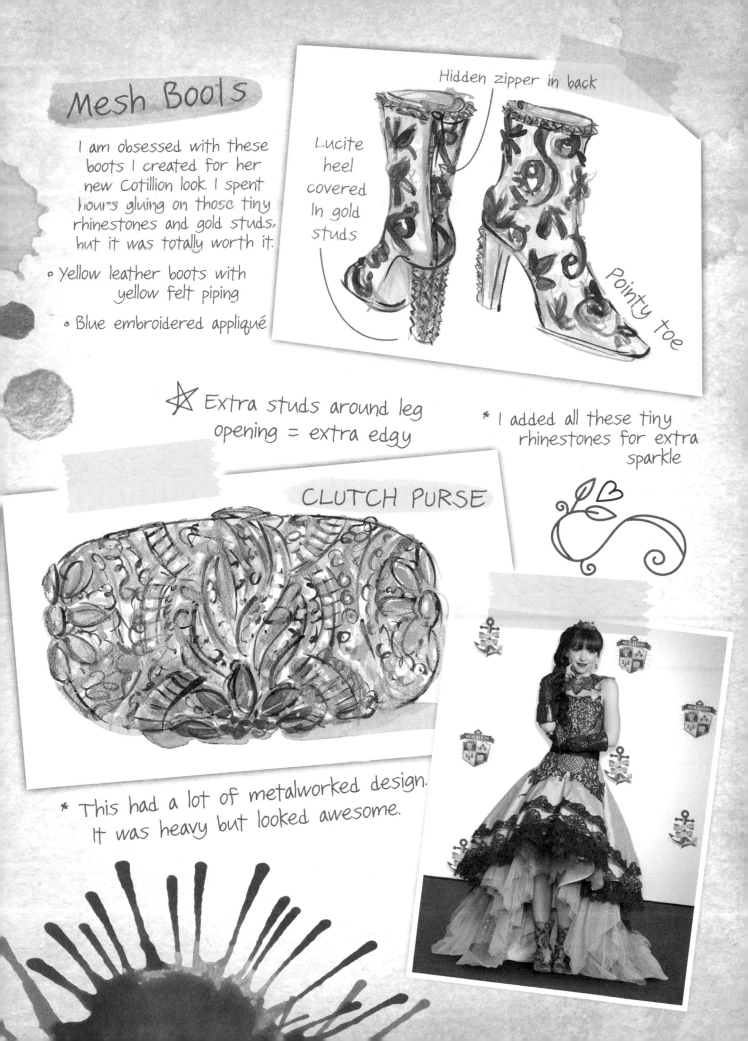

Uma showing up to Cotillion was unexpected (to say the least). Eventually everyone realized she had spelled Ben, making him fall in love with her so he'd bring down the barrier around the Isle. Mal was able to break the spell with True Love's Kiss, but that didn't stop Uma from seeking revenge. It was an intense night, but what I keep going back to is that moment when Mal transformed. I was filled with pride for my best friend. Not just for being brave enough to tell Ben that she loved him, but for being brave enough to face Uma as her truest self—the fierce dragon within. She was powerful and strong and totally in control, and I'd never seen her look more beautiful.

Mal's Magic Dress

Purple and black
embroidered collar

COTILLION CROWN
A headpiece fit for a queen.
This crown went perfectly with
Mal's magic gown.
- Emeralds
- Gold dragon charm
- Amethysts and diamonds

Black embroidery
on bodice

Green piping
at waist

Long fingerless
leather gloves

Layers of different
colored tulle create
a full skirt

* Purple,
black,
lavender

* Black train made from soft tulle

Some gowns are pure magic—literally. Mal conjured this up at Cotillion, and I wanted to save it in here because it's part of Auradon fashion history. Plus, I might be able to use it as inspiration for future designs. It's dark and brooding, feminine and edgy—I love it.

My business wouldn't be what it is if it wasn't for Doug's help.

We're such a good team, and we work so well together, that sometimes I take for granted that Doug is the sweetest, kindest guy I know. He cares so much about me. He wants me to be my best self, always, and he encourages me to dream bigger and bolder than I ever did before.

Sometimes, when we're delivering dresses together, he'll make me laugh so hard I get tears in my eyes. He surprises me with flowers he's picked from the meadow, or a cupcake he found in town that has the lemon icing I love. And he's always leaving me little notes and poems, just to remind me how much he cares. I'd need three sketchbooks to have room for all of them, but this is one of my favorites.

Evie + Doug 4ever

Your eyes
Like the sweetest chocolate
I could stare into them forever

Your skin
Like the softest silk
Please let me hold your hand in mine

Your mind
Like a roaring fire
Tell me what you're thinking

Your heart
Like the most beautiful sunset
I treasure the moments we're together

All of you is perfect

—Doug

Jane's Looks

It's really fun designing outfits for Jane, partly because her style is so different from mine. When I choose leather, she wants lace. When I want to layer with tights and jackets and scarves, she wants something simple and traditional—just a dress and heels. Working with Jane, I've learned a lot about really listening to my clients. (I've also incorporated classic Auradon style into more of my looks.)

MIXED FABRICS
White silk for collar
white silk at waist

Small bow at neckline

White lace ribbon
for sleeves

Jeweled detail
on belt

Light blue
textured lace
top

Embroidered silk with
beading for skirt

Because Jane is involved with so many school activities and on so many planning committees, I wanted to create something she could wear to different Auradon Prep events.

Lace edging on sleeves for a super feminine touch

Pale blue silk skirt

This party dress is a little more formal but can be dressed down by pairing it with flats and a simple white or blue cardigan.

Lonnie's School Dress

When Lonnie came to me asking for a casual everyday dress for school, I knew I had to do something interesting with the design. Lonnie is such a bright, positive person, I wanted her to shine in a unique, colorful outfit that no one else could wear.

Three straps in alternating colors

*Asymmetrical neckline

Single colorful sleeve in floral fabric

Subtle floral panel hidden on side

Pale blue piping along skirt seam

*Comfy, breathable cotton with a little stretch

*Pair with black high-heeled gladiator sandals

Lonnie isn't just one of the fiercest girls I know, she's one of the fiercest <u>people</u> I know.

Sometimes I think she's tougher than Carlos, Jay, and Chad combined. Like with what happened on the wharf. Mal and I were there, waiting to do battle with Uma and her pirates, when Lonnie jumped out of the limo right behind Carlos and Jay. Apparently, when Carlos and Jay were in their dorm room, she'd overheard them saying that Ben had been kidnapped. She wanted to come along to rescue him, and with all her training for R.O.A.R., she knew she would be valuable help. I was so relieved. I thought if anyone could hold their own in a sword fight against Harry Hook, it was Lonnie. It turns out I was right.

Even though Lonnie is obviously an amazing swordswoman, up until that point Jay hadn't been able to let her onto the R.O.A.R. team. There was some line in the rule book about the team being made up of a captain and eight men. So as soon as we got back to Auradon, he did the noble thing—he made Lonnie captain. I mean, he would've been crazy not to. What other Auradon Prep kid would be brave enough to come to the Isle? To fight a band of pirates . . . and win?

Lonnie's Athletic Outfit

* The top took me five days to sew, but it was totally worth it. I love how all the different fabric panels look together.

Floral fabric on the front
Turquoise netting on sleeves and front of jacket

*Black zipper

Soft, breathable cotton with stretch (Must be as comfortable as possible)

+ Black elastic at waist

Gray and blue leather gloves

Satin panel on one leg, for asymmetrical look

– Fuchsia satin trim for the pants

Now that Lonnie is captain of the R.O.A.R. team, she can't wear just any outfit to practice. And she's definitely not going to wear the boys' outfit. She came to me looking for something special.

Lonnie loved her training outfit so much that I decided to try my hand at designing athletic wear.

Athleisure Wear

Signature crown and heart

Wristbands for fashion and function

Satin-lined hood

*Tech fabric

Breathable
mesh

* For school
athletic
practices

Lightweight white sneakers
painted blue & gold

No collar
on jacket

*Dragon
appliqué on
front +
invisible zippers

Neoprene details

Ben's Classic Auradon Look

Ben is super preppy. Super "Auradon."

*Blue shirt with white collar and cuffs

Gold satin handkerchief

Royal blue lightweight wool jacket

Blue buttons

Slim-fit royal blue lightweight wool pants

When Ben told me he wanted to go to the Isle to find Mal, I knew he'd need backup.

Jay, Carlos, and I would have to help him. He'd also need a completely new (more villainous) look. Because everyone on the Isle dresses the same: worn, broken leather, painted over in places to hide the cracks and discoloration. Ripped scarves and slouchy hats. Pants that have been reinforced in the knees so they can be worn again and again. I pulled some of my favorite pieces together for him (some of which I had lying around), but that still didn't change the fact that Ben didn't act like an Isle kid. He still said please and thank you, and was walking around smiling at everyone. You can take the boy out of Auradon, but you can't take the Auradon out of the boy.

It wasn't long before people recognized him. Harry, Captain Hook's son, captured him. Uma and the other pirates held him for a night on their ship before my friends and I could get him back. If I could do it again, I would've designed a handkerchief or scarf to cover more of his face. I would've made him harder to recognize.

I guess, on the bright side (Fairy Godmother tells us to ALWAYS look on the bright side), at least he looked good when he was held captive!

The transformation to his "Chillin' like a villain" look...

* Hand-painted family crest on front

Black beanie cap

Studs on shoulders and arms (of course)

Gold leather piping on shoulder panels

Hand-painted gold accents on sleeves

Gold beast belt buckle

Blue leather fingerless gloves

Blue leather panels at knees

Embroidered gold appliqués on boot tongues

Ben's Isle Look

I think Ben looks great as an Isle kid!

Dear Evie,

I'm writing to express my sincerest gratitude for all you did for me when I was captured on the Isle. The situation was bad, but it could have been so much worse if you and your friends hadn't had the courage to fight back. I admire your bravery and determination.

You have become such a great example of all the potential and talent villain kids have to offer. It's been a true joy to watch you and your friends grow and change while at Auradon Prep, and to continue to see all the different ways you contribute to our community. Just yesterday, I looked around the quad and realized that over half the outfits I saw on students were Evie's 4 Hearts original designs. How cool.

Sincerely,
Ben

Maybe I've gotten a little soft since moving here, but this letter made my day. An official letter from the king!

Mal, Jay, Carlos, and I all got official letters from Ben, thanking us for our bravery on the Isle and for contributing so much to the community in our own unique ways. It feels good to know that people really appreciate us here. Maybe we'll always be villain kids, and we'll always be different—but that's what makes us special. That's what makes us . . . U.S.

I cannot believe what a whirlwind it's been. This fashion book represents who I was, and who I've become. . . and who I'm going to be. I'm glad I was able to take all of my sketches and photos and fashion ideas and put them all down into this book.

It just goes to show that when you love something and you work at it passionately, great things can happen. I started designing, and it became a mini-business, and now I'm being recognized by fashion magazines and the King of Auradon.

GOALS
(in no particular order)

- Sit down with Doug and make plans for growing my business

- Read books on History of Auradon Fashion (so much to learn!!)

- Take a Fashion Merchandising class

- Improve jewelry-making skills: techniques of knotting, weaving, and stringing with pearls and crystals

- Learn to make hats and headpieces

- Dizzy apprenticing me??

I want to savor this moment. And every time I look through these pages, I will. But, of course, I am thinking about what's next. I am so thrilled about what the future holds!

Rebel Attitude

#CotillionCouture

Rock this style!

Books + Fashion

=

MY HAPPY ENDING!

xoxo,
Evie